Rinpoche's Remarkable Ten-Week Weight Loss Clinic

by Roland Merullo

Rinpoche's Remarkable Ten-Week Weight Loss Clinic

PFP INC
publisher@pfppublishing.com
PO Box 829
Byfield, MA 01922

February 2016
Printed in the United States of America

ISBN-10:0-9970248-3-6
ISBN-13:978-0-9970248-3-8

Front Cover Photo
© Jonathan Kitchen - Getty Images

(also available in eBook format)

This is a work of fiction and not intended as a scientific weight loss program. While it might be of some help to those wrestling with eating problems and other addictions, it is intended simply as entertainment, not as medical advice. Readers with serious addiction or weight issues should contact professional counselors or a physician.

Also by Roland Merullo

Fiction

Leaving Losapas
A Russian Requiem
Revere Beach Boulevard
In Revere, In Those Days
A Little Love Story
Golfing with God
Breakfast with Buddha
American Savior
Fidel's Last Days
The Talk-Funny Girl
Lunch with Buddha
Vatican Waltz
Dinner with Buddha
The Delight of Being Ordinary

Non Fiction

Passion for Golf
Revere Beach Elegy
The Italian Summer: Golf, Food and Family at Lake Como
Demons of the Blank Page
Taking the Kids to Italy
The Ten Commandments of Golf Etiquette:
How to Make the Game More Enjoyable for Yourself
and for Everyone Else on the Course

For Jessica Lipnack

"Try, only try."
Zen Master Soehn Sahn Nim

Praise for Roland Merullo's Work

Leaving Losapas
"Dazzling . . . thoughtful and elegant . . . lyrical yet tough-minded . . . beautifully written, quietly brilliant."
— *Kirkus Reviews* [starred review]

A Russian Requiem
"Smoothly written and multifaceted, solidly depicting the isolation and poverty of a city far removed from Moscow and insightfully exploring the psyches of individuals caught in the conflicts between their ideals and their careers."
— *Publishers Weekly*

Revere Beach Boulevard
"Merullo invents a world that mirrors our world in all of its mystery. . . in language so happily inventive and precise and musical, and plots it so masterfully, that you are reluctant to emerge from his literary dream."
— *Washington Post Book World*

Passion for Golf: In Pursuit of the Innermost Game
"This accessible guide offers insight into the emotional stumbling blocks that get in the way of improvement and, most importantly, enjoyment of the game."
— *Publishers Weekly*

Revere Beach Elegy: A Memoir of Home and Beyond
"Merullo has a knack for rendering emotional complexities, paradoxes, or impasses in a mere turn of the phrase."
— *Chicago Tribune*

In Revere, In Those Days

"A portrait of a time and a place and a state of mind that has few equals."

— *The Boston Globe*

A Little Love Story

"There is nothing little about this love story. It is big and heroic and beautiful and tragic . . . Writing with serene passion and gentle humor, Merullo powerfully reveals both the resiliency and fragility of life and love . . . It is, quite utterly, grand."

— *Booklist*

Golfing with God

"Merullo writes such a graceful, compassionate and fluid prose that you cannot resist the characters' very real struggles and concerns . . . Do I think Merullo is a fine, perceptive writer who can make you believe just about anything? Absolutely."

— *Providence Journal*

Breakfast with Buddha

"Merullo writes with grace and intelligence and knows that even in a novel of ideas it's not the religion that matters, it's the relationship. . . It's a quiet, meditative, and ultimately joyous trip we're on."

— *Boston Globe*

Fidel's Last Days

"A fast-paced and highly satisfying spy thriller . . . Merullo takes readers on a fictional thrill ride filled with so much danger and drama that they won't want it to end."

— *Boston Globe*

American Savior

"Merullo gently satirizes the media and politics in this thoughtful commentary on the role religion plays in America. This book showcases Merullo's conviction that Jesus' real message about treating others with kindness is being warped by those who believe they alone understand the Messiah."
— *USA Today*

The Italian Summer: Golf, Food & Family at Lake Como

"This travel memoir delivers unadulterated joy . . . [Merullo's] account of those idyllic weeks recalls Calvin Trillin in its casual tone, good humor, affable interactions with family, and everyman's love of regional food and wine . . . A special travel book for a special audience."
— *Booklist*

The Talk-Funny Girl

"Merullo not only displays an inventive use of language in creating the Richards' strange dialect but also delivers a triumphant story of one lonely girl's resilience in the face of horrific treatment."
— *Booklist*

Lunch with Buddha

"A beautifully written and compelling story about a man's search for meaning that earnestly and accessibly tackles some well-trodden but universal questions. A quiet meditation on life, death, darkness and spirituality, sprinkled with humor, tenderness and stunning landscapes."
— *Kirkus* [starred review]

Vatican Waltz

"Merullo's latest is a page-turning novel of religious ideas written with love and imagination. . . With fillips of *The Da Vinci Code* conspiracy and *Eat Pray Love* gourmandism, this book will speak loudly to Catholic readers . . . It also sings with finely observed details of family relationships, ethnic neighborhood life, and the life of prayer. The shoulda-seen-it-coming ending is a miracle . . ."
— *Publishers Weekly* [starred review]

The Ten Commandments of Golf Etiquette: How to Make the Game More Enjoyable for Yourself and for Everyone Else on the Course

"Golf, a magnificent addiction for the initiated, can be a mystery for newcomers hoping to pick it up. Roland Merullo's *The Ten Commandments of Golf Etiquette* is the Rosetta Stone for anyone looking to break through the game's clutter of rules and protocols. It combines Merullo's passion for golf with his gift for clear writing, humor and insight."
—Tim Murphy, retired Senior Editor, *Golf World*

Dinner with Buddha

"We, like Otto, find our cynicism worn away by Rinpoche's gentle instruction in the simple but terribly difficult art of letting go, living each moment to the fullest, seeing the sacred in the everyday . . .Sharp character sketches of people encountered on the way and occasional references to current events keep the narrative from floating away in spiritual self-absorption. . .Clearly there's more to come. With six unconventionally religious novels to date, this brave, meditative author has carved a unique niche in American literature."
— *Kirkus* [starred review]

*Rinpoche's Remarkable Ten-Week
Weight Loss Clinic*

- 1 -

I was in a good mood on that day, about to enjoy a celebratory meal with my brother-in-law, the famous spiritual master, Volya Rinpoche. We were sitting opposite each other at a small table in my favorite pizza place, Amadeo's, in the West Village, and Rinpoche—as everyone called him—was holding his almost-full beer mug in one fist and gazing at me with a species of absolute approval I'd seen from him many times. It warmed me. It made me remember certain things he'd said over the course of his memorable weight-loss clinic.

For the purposes of that clinic—which had its first meeting on a frigid Saturday morning in early January—he'd rented a room from a friend who ran a yoga studio on the west side of Ninth Avenue, near Twentieth Street. The room had tall windows facing onto the Avenue, an abundance of light, and he'd brought in a few dozen folding chairs because he assumed—correctly in my case—that the people who'd signed up for his clinic weren't the type to be comfortable sitting cross-legged on a yoga mat. Rinpoche, of course, could have sat like that all day, legs crossed, one small black cushion under his wide rear end. But that would have made the rest of us feel even worse than we already felt about ourselves, and I'm sure my kind brother-in-law knew that, and so he sat in a folding chair facing us, the gold-trimmed maroon robe hanging down around his bare brown feet, his hands held loosely together in his lap, spine straight but not rigidly straight, his shaved head shining and his face lit with what can only be described as the joy of being alive. He wasn't smiling, though. In fact, if you didn't know him well, you might have thought his closed lips and square, rough-looking face belonged to a man about to deliver a stern lecture on overeating, on self-discipline, on taking control of your messed-up life.

But that wasn't Rinpoche's style. A more-or-less Buddhist master of indeterminate age, he had meditation centers scattered across the globe, had written several best-selling books before marrying my beautiful sister, and generally devoted his life to bringing others the kind of peace he seemed to have been born with. He did have a forceful side, but he was more often kind, understanding, comically compassionate.

"This not a course in Buddhism," he began, on that morning, squeezing his fingers in a gentle flex and running his eyes around the room. "But to me is interesting that, in Buddhist kind of thinking you have two ways to look on life. Absolute way and Relative way." He had a ceramic mug beside him on a small table—green tea—and he paused and sipped the tea, moving it around in his mouth, working his lips, setting the mug back in its place and finally swallowing and looking at his audience again. Twenty-four souls of various colors and ages had responded to the ad he'd placed in a Manhattan magazine, all of us twenty to a hundred-and-twenty pounds heavier than we wished to be.

"In the Absolute view, you are perfect now, this minute." He glanced sternly at each of us as if ready to argue with anyone who dared dispute this statement. "Perfect," he repeated, forcefully. "Nothing wrong with your body, nothing wrong with your face, nothing wrong even with the things you done so far in this life. Nothing. Who doesn't think this is true?"

My guess is that no one in the room thought it was true, but such was the force of the man's belief in what he was saying, so sure and clear was his voice, that no one raised a hand. We were all perfect. For half a second maybe some of us even believed that.

"Good!" Rinpoche said, and then the stern wall of his face broke apart and he laughed. Chuckled might be a better word, an elegant riff of small puffs of amusement, of appreciation for the fact that all of us were sitting there, basically starting things off on a false note by not raising our hands. "Good!" he repeated. Another thoughtful sip of tea. "And then, Relative view. Who knows what is?"

A very large redheaded woman in the first row raised her hand and when he nodded at her she said, "In the relative way we're all fat."

Rinpoche threw back his head and laughed, an uproarious laugh this time, abundant joy. Not exactly the kind of reaction you'd expect in a traditional weight-loss clinic. But 'traditional' wasn't a label that fit the man. He was a monk, yes, but even his Buddhism—of Tibetan lineage via a south-Siberian upbringing—did not quite graze within the customary pastures of that faith. He nodded, let the laugh play itself out in another small run of chuckling. "Fat, fat," he said, moving one hand in circles along his tight belly. "This is why we here, yes?"

"Yes!" a half dozen people answered, and for a few seconds they—we—seemed to be, if not exactly happy about being overweight, then at least not tormented by it, not carrying around with us, in addition to the extra poundage, the harsh judgments of our fanatical society, the years of insults, real or imagined, external and internal. Every celebrity, every sporting event, every advertisement, every magazine cover—all of it conspired to form an ongoing taunt. We were chubby, plump, overweight, fat, obese, semi-disgusting. We should be ashamed.

"So now what we goin' to do these ten week," Rinpoche went on, "is we goin' to take the Absolute and make it so the Relative matches up and looks to us almost same, okay? You listen to me exactly. You do what I say exactly. Ten week from now, if you still feel the Relative way you don't pay zero! If you feel the Absolute way maybe you go out for pizza and the beer with Rinpoche, okay? Any question?"

The same woman in the front row raised her hand. "Sir," she began, "with all respect, I have been fat for as long as I can remember. Thirty years. Forty years maybe. Before I started school I was fat. And in two and a half months I won't be? That seems impossible."

"Maybe so," Rinpoche admitted. "Ten week not much time, you right. Maybe we fail." He laughed again, as if the idea of failure was so unlikely that it amused him. "But maybe we talk, you and me, when we finish and we see how you doin', okay?"

She nodded skeptically, and there was a skeptical stirring in the room. I could feel it in myself. It sounded ridiculously too good to be true. Even the modest fee—two hundred dollars for those who could afford it; half that or less for those who could not, paid not upon enrollment but upon completion—seemed, at that moment, like part of a scam. I knew Rinpoche well, knew, first-hand, all the good he'd done. And if I suspected a scam. . . . . I looked around the room at the other faces. A mix of hopefulness and cynicism. Over the decades of our plumpness there had been so many promises like this, one diet after the next, books, clinics, weight-loss gurus, exercise classes, Zumba, yoga, South Beach, Mediterranean, Paleo, a few weeks or a few months of success and then, all-too-familiar failure. We wanted to believe, but our histories, our very bodies, stood as evidence in the case against belief.

A short, stocky man with a salt-and-pepper goatee, a man I would come to think of as "Obnoxious Joe" made a "hmphing" sound from the left side of the room and whispered, loudly enough to be heard by all of us, "Another fraud, you ask me."

Rinpoche didn't seem to hear. "We start now," he said, "with small meditation. Five minutes only. Impossible to fail in meditation, okay?"

"Impossible to fail?" a man sitting near me said in a sad voice. "I've tried so many times! I close my eyes and my mind goes crazy on me. I can't do it, Rinpoche!"

Rinpoche looked at him, eyebrows raised, face rippling with empathy. "You can't fail!" he repeated. "Meditation doesn't mean mind goes blank, means only that you look at it. You stop putting things into it for a few minutes and you look what happens, okay? If you think, "I'm failing! I can't do!" then you look at that. Just look, okay?"

"Okay," the man said, but without enthusiasm.

"Now, five minutes we close the eyes and sit and watch mind. No questions afterwards. This is not the test for you in school, okay?"

We sat there. After running in circles for a few minutes around Obnoxious Joe and all the things I had always wanted to say to people like him, my mind swung back to the days when my wife had been alive, my kids at home, my job secure instead of non-existent. I'd been a senior editor at a respected publishing house that specialized, ironically enough, in books on food. I loved food, loved to try new dishes from the international spectrum of culinary delight, the cornucopia of Manhattan's eating places. And to compensate, I'd exercised regularly—an hour a day at the gym in winter, long walks and jogs and multiple games of tennis in the warmer months. I hadn't been svelte since my college hockey-playing days, since our first few years of marriage. Even trim might have been an exaggeration for most of the previous twenty years. But, unless you were staring at my belly on the beach you wouldn't have noticed my weight. I barely noticed it. I was more or less in shape for a man my age. It wasn't an issue. And then, after a series of life's hardest blows, it was.

So my mind went there—to my late wife, Jeannie, to the feeling of her hands on my skin, the sound of her voice, to the love of my son and daughter, to work, and then to the dissolution: her diagnosis and long suffering, my kids leaving home for the challenges and joys of adulthood, my boss firing me via email, the lonely evenings on the couch in Bronxville in front of the TV with a bottle of red wine and take-out Italian, cookies and ice cream for dessert. And, in the morning, a kind of hangover, the sour, wet blanket of regret, the mirror as enemy, the clothes that no longer fit, the feeling of my belly drooping toward the tops of my thighs when I sat. For breakfast I'd have a cinnamon roll or a frosted raisin scone, as if that might ease the pain.

The meditation—no wonder people avoided it— had brought me into the territory of self-loathing. Rinpoche rang his little bell and sighed and we opened our eyes and looked at him.

"Okay. First part finish. Every day you do this. Five minutes. One rule: if you feel a thought you don't like, you say, "Hah! There is thought." You don't push it away, you try not let it upset you. You watch, okay? No failure."

Another sip of tea, another contemplative swallow, another compassionate surveying of the room. "Now, here is assignment. You take a partner now, okay? You and this partner talk little bit. You both of you choosing one food you eat that helps make you carry the too much weight, okay? Maybe is ice cream, maybe candy, maybe bread, maybe the wine or the beer or the potato. Only one. This week you don't eat that food. Also, you eat maybe ninety percents of the food you usually eat. Just make the dish ten percents more smaller if you eating at home. In a restaurant, maybe this means you waste little bit. Okay, usually we try not to waste, but not so bad to waste little bit for this week. It goes back in the earth, that food. You give up one thing, you eat ninety percents, and you meditate five minutes, okay?"

"Seems way too easy," a young woman said from the middle of the room.

"Maybe not so easy when you do it. Plus, you walk one mile every day. Only one, not two. Walk, not run. Rain, snow, hot, you feel tired—doesn't matter, you walk, okay? And when you sitting down at work every maybe one hour you stand up and move a little. The stretches, the walking around. That's all. No questions now. No arguments from you. Everybody understand?"

Nods all around, a few frowns and twisted lips. I could hear people thinking: and for this I'm paying two hundred bucks! But no one said a word.

"Go now," Rinpoche said. "My perfect friends."

- 2 -

It wasn't, of course, as easy as it sounded. Habits, even the smallest habits, are etched into the essence of who we are, and breaking them is like unscratching a scratched eyeglass lens. But I tried. My partner was Edna, a friendly woman from Jersey City. We sat together after the class ended, exchanged phone numbers and email addresses, and a little personal information. Edna was probably more than eighty pounds overweight, an African American professor of Chemistry at a Manhattan University, and widowed mother of four grown boys. She seemed like a happy woman, but I noticed that it was a struggle for her to stand, and when she walked across the room I could see that every day must be a struggle for her. Why wouldn't a person like that decide to take solace in eating?! If every hour was that painful, if people were constantly looking at her, if she could read their thoughts— F—A—T printed on their eyeballs—why wouldn't she seek some comfort in the innocent pleasure of food?

It was ice cream for her. Coffee ice cream. Sundaes, ice cream sodas, shakes. Two or three or sometimes four a day, she confessed sadly. She had her favorite places—near the university where she taught—and she had an entire stash in a freezer at home. For me, I decided, perhaps too ambitiously, it was wheat in all its glorious forms. Scones, pasta, pizza crusts, garlic bread, a fresh baguette from the French bakery near my house, slathered in butter and taken with a glass of wine. Toast in the morning, a sandwich at lunch, pasta Bolognese for dinner with a cookie or three afterwards. Wheat would be the food I gave up.

"That sounds like a lot," Edna said, and I nodded in a proud way. I was up to the challenge. I was familiar with Rinpoche's methods and, really, I told myself, by the standards of that room, I was barely eligible for the clinic.

But, as things turned out, it wasn't so easy. The walk, the ninety-percent rule—no problem. But having coffee in the morning without toast, or passing the bakery and not stepping inside for a loaf of country white or sourdough sesame, or sitting down to lunch with a friend and ignoring the twenty-seven different sandwiches on the menu and on the plates around us, or having a burger without the bun. . . not easy at all. But for that first week, by a moderate exertion of will, I managed it. Rinpoche had instructed us not to weigh ourselves, but even without a number as proof I knew the program was working. I climbed the stairs to the second meeting of his clinic feeling lighter. Victorious.

- 3 -

I sat next to Edna. She had streaks of tears down both cheeks. Before Rinpoche began to speak she leaned her mouth close to my ear and whispered, "I was doing so well and then I stopped for a coffee milkshake on the way over here! What is wrong with me, Otto?!"

I put my hand on her soft arm and squeezed once, but before I could say anything Rinpoche opened the meeting. "This like meditation, this first week," he said. "This is not like the test in school, the exmamination. . . Exmamination, right?" He looked at me. I shrugged, smiled. He laughed at himself and said, "Not like the test! You cannot fail this first week, you see? What happened so far, all okay. Good practice. Now we try the next week. First, eight minutes sitting, instead of five. Close eyes now. No failure."

This time my restless mind moved around and around from my children to the sounds on the street, from Edna's teary face to my seven-day triumph, paltry as it was. Some sly voice kept whispering: no failure! So if you had slipped, if you'd eaten, say, just one or two cookies, Rinpoche would feel the same way about you,

11

correct? No failure! I was perfect exactly as I was! What a wonderful idea.

The bell rang. I looked up guiltily to find Rinpoche staring at me. He seemed, as he often did, to be reading my mind. I'd spent the week alone in my too-large Bronxville home—he was staying in the city for a month with a traveling group of Tibetan monastic singers—but I had the sense he'd been watching me through some psychic periscope. Now he raised his thin brows and held his eyes on me. Conscience incarnated.

No failure! I was thinking. I'm perfect the way I am. . . . But it wasn't quite working.

"No failure," Rinpoche the mind-reader said. "On the Absolute level. But, you know, we want, on the Relative level, to make a small change. This small change, it takes the work. The work it needs the little bit of pain, maybe, or not pain, maybe energy. So now we take a breath to bring in that energy into our self and we try. This week now you give up the food again, this same food. Seven day. Really try now, okay? Plus the ninety percents rule. Maybe even eighty-eight percents!" He laughed. "Plus the one mile walk now is one and a half mile. And the meditation is not five minutes in the morning only but in the night, too. Wery simple but maybe not that easy. When you want to give up, you call the partner, yes? And plus I want that one time this week, you pick the one time, but one time you eat just water for one meal, maybe breakfast is easier, maybe lunch, up to you. Okay?"

He looked around the room in a way that encouraged questions, and a woman who'd been silent the previous week raised her arm. "Can we eat between meals?" she asked.

"Maybe water or tea between meals. Or maybe one small fruit, okay? Or a piece of vegetables."

She nodded. Obnoxious Joe was next. All of five-foot-three, he stood up so as to make a larger impression. The instant he was on his feet a gushing river of vitriol poured forth: that this was a scam; that he'd done some research and Rinpoche had no credentials as a nutritionist; that he'd been to many, many weight-loss clinics and none of them had been anything remotely like this; that there wasn't enough of a specific blueprint for what he was supposed to do; there were no calories being measured; and on and on in the harshest tones.

Rinpoche watched him patiently. The expression on his face did not change. Joe had his full attention and when, after a minute or perhaps a minute and a half, he finally ran out of gas, Rinpoche nodded. Took a sip of tea. Said, in a pleasant voice, "That is all?" and a few people laughed. Obnoxious Joe did not. Rinpoche nodded again. "You say some things that are true," he told him. "And you cannot have to pay, if you want, at the end. The money goes to the food pantry anyways. Rinpoche has plenty." More laughter. "But I think maybe you should try this method one or two more week because all the other times didn't work so good— you said this, not me—and sometimes when things don't work we try new things, okay?"

Joe sat down without answering and kept watching Rinpoche skeptically, bitterly, lips pressed together. I took so much pleasure in my silent criticism of him.

"I think you have a lot of the anger in you," Rinpoche went on, looking directly into Joe's eyes. "That's okay. Okay to be anger sometimes. Flustration, too, maybe."

"Frustration," Joe corrected. "Yes, exactly. With you. With this."

"And maybe a little bit with something else, too," Rinpoche said, gently. "You cannot come back here if you don't want, and I understand, but I say try maybe two more week and see."

No one else had any questions or comments, but Joe's fiery words seemed to have had an effect on the room, as if a tide were turning against Rinpoche, a silent tide of resistance. I sensed it in the facial expressions and eye movement. I could feel it in myself, I could hear it in the whispering, tempting voice. Perfect as you are! No nutritional qualifications!

A propaganda of cookies and cake.

"Watch," Rinpoche said, "when you have the temptation to eat this one food that you giving up, watch the way the thinking works for that, okay? Goin' to be a little voice saying you want a potato, or you want more than the ninety percents. Or you don't want meditate. Or you don't want the walk. If you find that voice inside the busy mind, just look on it. That is the beginning to make the change, okay? See you next week."

- 4 -

I did everything Rinpoche told us to do. I did not eat so much as a crumb of white flour. Portionwise, I went to about eighty-five percent of what I would usually consume. I meditated (an activity that, thanks to my famous brother-in-law's influence, had already been a part of my life for years) I stood up from my desk on a regular basis. Cold January rain and weak winter sun, I took the mile and a half walk, and instead of breakfast on Wednesday I had four glasses of water.

I mentioned all this, in passing, in a modest way, when I spoke with my son and daughter by phone during the week. I accepted their congratulations. For a while I felt solid, confident, a new man.

But, at the same time, since I was feeling a bit lighter on my feet, I twice treated myself to a chocolate milkshake in the ice cream parlor in town. (I did not mention that to Tasha or Anthony). I justified this with the argument that I was obeying the rules, otherwise. That I was going to tell Edna what I'd done. . . . only in order to make her feel less badly about herself. That it was fair.

I knew, of course, that it wasn't fair at all, and that

my sneaking a milkshake—two of them actually—would do nothing to help Edna and might even hurt her. I knew it. But that knowing was buried beneath something else, a layer of a certain kind of logic, a rationalization. For a few minutes after each of those milkshakes I felt fine, proud of myself even. It was all right. There was no failure. I was perfect just as I was, a free man. But then, an hour or two hours later, or sometimes the next morning, the sour feeling seeped back in. It was wrong. I was cheating. I went for an extra-long walk.

- 5 -

Over the third and fourth weeks the basic pattern repeated itself. Rinpoche was kind, forgiving, but firm. Five people quit the program, including the redheaded woman. Obnoxious Joe stayed on. Two or three others complained out loud, but also stayed. Edna and I took to speaking on the phone even when we weren't particularly tempted to cheat on the diet. In late afternoon one of us would call the other and we'd talk for a bit, sometimes not even about food. Sometimes she'd call while she was walking and I could hear what a struggle it was for her. A mile and a half walk, she said, took her the better part of an hour. She found the meditations fairly comfortable, which was strange, I told her, because I'd been meditating for some years by then, but the new dietary rules seemed to have caused tremors in my interior world. The meditations—which had grown easier and easier over time—were uproarious again. "I can almost hear the competing voices," I said. "That little whisper telling me one slice of pizza won't matter."

"That's a good sign, I think," she said. "It's important. Most of us can't hear that whisper yet."

Probably it was important, but, at the same time, between the fourth and fifth meetings I faced a crisis out of all proportion to the amount of sacrifice I was making. All of a sudden it became imperative for me to have just one piece of toast with my breakfast eggs. The voice wasn't whispering anymore, it was shouting. Toast in the morning, it said, and then, later, just one cookie—just one—or a slice of pizza. I couldn't walk from the train station to my house, a route that took me past Sean's Greek Style Pizza (not joking), without this evil voice screaming in my ear, reminding me of the oily slice of onion and sausage I was missing out on, and what difference would it make—one slice— and wasn't it true that I'd moved the belt buckle up a notch, and didn't that mean I could afford a slice now and again? And there wasn't much bread involved in a slice of pizza anyway, it was mainly protein and vegetables, and most people had given up one food, not a whole category. And on and on.

One time I actually stepped into Sean's, determined to break my fast and declare my independence. Fortunately, there were three people in front of me in line and, fortunately, after the first of them had been served I felt myself reaching into my pocket for my phone. I called Edna and she said, "Walk out! Now! Just do it. Walk out, Otto!" and I did, and I thanked her and she said, "I owed you."

- 6 -

On the occasion of our fifth meeting Rinpoche said, "We now gone almost half the way to the end!" and he ran his eyes over us as if we were all succeeding beautifully. We had the willpower of monks. We couldn't fail. "Now, maybe, you try little bit more hard, okay? Now you give up the second food that causing trouble. You stay at one and half mile. You stay at eighty-eight percents. But you give up food number two and you meditate ten minute morning and five night, okay?"

"How many foods are we going to give up eventually?" a hugely obese man asked quietly. It seemed clear to me—and maybe to him, as well—that he'd have to give up eating altogether for months, and walk miles and miles and miles to have any hope of changing his profile even slightly. His eyes were tiny marbles in purses of pink flesh. His middle drooped halfway to his knees. I couldn't imagine how he made his way through the world, how he bought clothes, what his blood pressure must be, how much he must suffer over the course of any given day. "I gave up all sugar, Rinpoche, but I can think of another five foods, at least, that con-

19

tribute to the problem."

"I think maybe two only," Rinpoche said. "But we do some other things. Important to choose the two biggest foods that make the problem now, but more important to do the meditation ten and five minutes, okay?"

"For me the so-called meditation is just thinking. My mind is like a car going a hundred miles an hour. I think and think and the alarm goes off and nothing else has happened."

"Wery good!" Rinpoche said. A woman behind me snorted. "But have one thing to bring the mind back to, okay? At the start you choose this thing. Breath, maybe. Or some words. "Jesus have mercy on me," some people like to say if they Christian. Or 'Peace'. Or 'Quiet'. Or come back to one face that loved you in your life. Or one, how you say, one picture in your mind."

"An image."

"Yes, inage. The mind go and go and you come back to this inage. Don't get upset if the mind go many minutes before you find that it is going. Just come back without being upset. The breath, the body, the inage. You choose, but stay with this one thing every day. Plus two foods, plus the walk. Plus the eighty-eight percents."

"I'm noticing," another man said from the back of the room, "that I don't have quite the same urge I used to have for the food I gave up. Which was all junk food, by the way. Chips, cookies, candy. I decided it was all a single category and I gave it up and, though there are still moments when I have an urge, the urge is smaller. The one time I slipped, the taste itself was less pleasant."

Several people in front of me were nodding.

"I haven't gotten there," I found myself saying, as if to balance this report from the field. The words had just erupted. "I'd love to get there. It's wheat for me— bread and scones and cookies and pasta. Another category, I guess. But when I walk by the bakery on the way home from the train station my mouth actually waters."

"Choose another route home," someone called from the far side of the room.

"Yes, that's what I do," someone else said.

I nodded, chastened. It was such a simple solution, but something had stood between me and it. There was some kind of invisible obstacle in the logical progression of thought from problem to solution. Addiction, was the right name for that obstacle, but it had always seemed too strong a word to be applied to me.

The room fell into silence. I ran my eyes around my colleagues and counted. We were down to seventeen. Three of them, including Edna and the man who'd just spoken, were in a category that could be described by the word—obese. One or two of them looked like they needed to lose only about ten to fifteen pounds. The rest were my colleagues in the twenty-to-forty-pound category, pinched between the hopeless, or, at least, the ones who seemed to me to have no real hope of success short of surgery, and the confident, the ones who, even if they failed completely would not really suffer very much. I guessed there were probably something like a hundred million Americans in this clinic with us. We were a nation burdened with excess poundage and all the shame that went along with it. A whole weight-loss industry had spawned from the dirty waters of this shame. How had this happened?

- 7 -

That week Edna and I decided to meet for lunch. We chose a Chinese restaurant, because there wasn't much in the way of tempting wheat products on the menu, and the chances were slim that they served coffee ice cream. I don't know how Edna felt with me, but I was slightly worried about eating in front of her, given what we were going through together, so I ordered what seemed to me the healthiest available option: chicken with mixed vegetables. She pondered the menu for a few minutes, then one-upped me: chicken with steamed vegetables. While we waited for the food to be served, she stared out the window. Sadly, it seemed, and I studied her.

She was an unusually attractive woman, with bright eyes and a lively mouth and, somewhat guiltily, I tried to picture what she'd look like if she lost the excess pounds. Truly beautiful, I decided. And I suppose that made it worse for her, that at one point in her life she'd walked through the world carrying a very different sense of herself, and that sense had been encouraged and supported by a dozen daily encounters: envious looks from other women, admiring looks from men, people of both sexes complimenting her, thin TV celebrities unthreatening.

"You seem sad," I said, without knowing I would say it.

She turned her eyes to me and tilted her head slightly to one side. "A little bit," she said, "today." Our waiter brought a pot of tea and two cups and Edna waited for him to pour and leave before continuing. "Today would have been our thirtieth wedding anniversary. Ron and I."

"I'm sorry."

A sad smile. "I guess the saddest part is that he died mainly from being overweight. I was slim when I met him, and he was always a little on the heavy side, a big football star in college, a lineman. After I had each of our children I gained a few pounds, but over those years he gained a lot more, and kept gaining and gaining. I tried to talk to him a hundred times. Even the boys tried, when they got older. He'd get angry, say he had a lot of responsibility—which was true. One time he even lost control and told the boys he'd been fine before they were born, and it was the responsibility of having children that had made him fat. He apologized later, felt terrible about it for years. The doctors went after him about the weight, I went after him—a little too hard sometimes. Nothing worked. And so, I think, after a while, I started to eat to keep him company, or because it was too lonely watching what I ate when he didn't, or because I couldn't bear to have him feel so bad about himself in comparison to me."

"An empathy of overeating," I said.

Edna nodded, brightening a bit. "It worked, too, in a way. I don't think he felt as bad about himself for the last few years. But his heart couldn't take a load like that. There was a part of him that still thought like an athlete. Some nights he walk up the stairs fast, as if he were remembering the days when he could run. He'd do that at work, too, I guess—his office was on the third floor, and some days he'd decide he just wasn't going to take the elevator—and one of those times his heart gave out and they found him sprawled on his face on the stairwell, gone."

"I'm very sorry. I know what it's like. It makes a hole in the world that can't be filled."

"And from then on I found that I couldn't stop, couldn't go back to the way I'd eaten before. Part of me didn't want to."

"How old were your children?"

"From fourteen to twenty-three at that point."

"Sad."

"The fourteen-year-old is twenty-two now. At college. Getting fat like Mom."

"I'm very sorry."

She nodded, "And you?" she said, after a moment. "Tell you the truth, I don't even see why you're in the program. I wish I had the amount of fat on me that you have on you."

"Thanks, I guess."

We both laughed. The food was served. I told Edna my own story, the losses, the new lethargy. "Plus,

Rinpoche's my brother-in-law, and that was part of the motivation. When he mentioned the clinic idea—completely out of the blue—I immediately volunteered."

"One strange creature," she said.

"Wonderful, though, in so many ways."

"I'm liking the meditation stuff, though I think that would be the hardest part for most people, and I can't really say I understand how it connects to losing weight."

"He insists it's the mind that makes us fat. That if we could trace things back to the moment when the mind says "Eat this!" we could see that we had a choice."

"Happens too fast for me," Edna said.

"Me, too, but I trust him. He's helped me in so many other ways—with the grief, with anger, just made me feel different."

We began to eat, reminding each other, in a joking way, that we'd been ordered to waste twelve per cent of what was on the plate.

"My mother grew up hungry," Edna said, between bites. "That's the other part of it, I think. She'd been hungry as a girl, so wasting food was a sin in our house, a literal sin."

We ate in silence for a while, carefully leaving a bit of food on the plate, filling the empty space in our bellies with tea, avoiding each other's eyes. When the waiter came and removed the plates, we sat over tea and fortune cookies (which, I convinced myself, were not made with flour. Mine said, "New encounters will teach you." Edna wouldn't tell me hers.) We split the bill and while waiting for change, she said, "Do you think I'm attractive?"

"Very attractive. Yes."

"You're not just saying that?"

"It's funny," I said. "In some strange way I feel like we can't lie to each other. It's as if, because we both went into a room and admitted we had a problem, we've taken a truth serum. I think, probably, in your youth you were gorgeous."

Her eyes filled and I realized, too late, that it had been a foolish thing to say. She dabbed at them with the napkin and looked away, then back. "I wasn't coming on to you, you know. Lonely as my life is, I'm not hinting for a date or anything. I just. . . it's just that I used to feel. . . not gorgeous, but sexy, appealing, attractive. For years I felt that way. Now I feel like a monster. I scare little kids when I walk into a room. My students make doodles of me that resemble whales. I saw one, once, left behind on the desk."

"You seem to feel good about yourself."

"An act," she said. "You wouldn't understand."

"No, in fact, I would. If there were a number attached to my own self-esteem, say, on a scale of 100, then I'd guess my score goes down one or two points for every pound I'm overweight. But I've become good at pretending otherwise, wearing loose sweaters and hiding my belly in family photos."

"Do you think his program will work? It seems impossible. I mean, I know I've lost some, but the amount I need to lose, the amount some of those people in the room need to lose, you can't possibly do that in ten weeks."

"Agreed," I said. "I'm hoping I get a set of ....'tools' for lack of a better word, that I can keep using until I feel fairly good about myself again."

"You give me hope, saying that. And don't worry, I'm not going to nudge you into asking me out or anything. I shouldn't have put you on the spot like that. I'm sorry."

I made a joke then, something about having been out of the dating world for so long and being so out of practice that I felt I'd gone into permanent retirement.

We left a nice tip and made our way toward the door, Edna struggling to move between the close-set tables, and breathing hard once we were out on the sidewalk. A few snowflakes drifted down and melted on the tops of parked cars. "Well, thank you," she said. "For being my partner, for all your help."

"Thank you right back," I told her, and we went off in opposite directions, Edna to the college, and yours truly to the Grand Central for the short ride home. Sitting on the train, staring out at Harlem, the Bronx, and then the first dusting of snow on suburban lawns, I felt a subtle peace surrounding me. A new encounter, as the cookie had predicted. A new friend.

- 8 -

In the days following our sixth meeting I discovered a newfound respect for the other people in the clinic, for the ones, like Edna, who'd been wrestling with weight issues for so much longer than I had. I believe this happened because, in those days, I was walking through what seemed to me one of the outer circles of dietary hell, simply from having given up a favorite food for five weeks. I dreamt about bread. I woke up thinking about food. I took a walking route that led nowhere near the bakery or Sean's and yet those places seemed to have moved into the center of my world, as if men with flour-dusted hands had taken up residence in my kitchen. The frozen pizzas at the market—a food-like item that had formerly tempted me about as much as a trip to the Sudan for a half-marathon in summer—now seemed to be singing "Otto! Otto, my friend!" as soon as I parked my car in the lot.

And I was trying to lose twenty pounds, not a hundred.

And this was my first serious attempt at public weight loss, not my fifth or fifteenth.

I called Edna and said, "I thought that, after a while, we were supposed to lose the urge for whatever it is we're giving up."

"I know!" she agreed, and I could tell by the tone of her exclamation, even over the phone, that she was going through the same kind of fires that were singeing my skin. "I threw out my stores of ice cream—four half-gallons—but last night I got out of bed and went to the freezer to see if maybe a little bit had leaked out and I might scoop it up and lick the spoon! Can you believe that? It feels like every cell in my body is chanting: "Coffee ice cream! Coffee ice cream!""

"We're supposed to just look at that, just see it, acknowledge it."

"Well, I see it anyway. That much I can manage.. . . sometimes."

"That's supposed to be a start."

"What's worse, and something Rinpoche hasn't talked about, is that I've turned into a bitch. I keep most of it inside, but a couple of times at work I've snapped at people—my secretary, for one. I never snap at her. In fourteen years I've never snapped at her. I apologized four times and bought her a box of candy. So what happens? She offers me a piece from the box!"

"Did you take it?"

"I took it. And then I wrapped it in a napkin so she wouldn't see and threw it in the wastebasket."

"That seems like progress."

"Sure, Otto, but if I have to choose between being fat or being bitchy, well, I don't know. Fat's starting to seem not so bad."

"I'm in the same boat," I admitted, "but I don't have co-workers anymore, and no one has been living here, so I'm somewhat protected."

"You sound like the same, pleasant man."

"You don't see me in private."

"You're too hard on yourself."

"That's part of our problem, isn't it?"

When I hung up the phone I sank down on the leather sofa. The part about living alone was true, but it was going to be true only for another day. Rinpoche's monk-friends were leaving town and he'd asked if he could come and stay with me for the remaining weeks before heading back to his family and the retreat center in North Dakota. So whatever wiggle room I might have had, whatever opportunity to cheat, or semi-cheat, would be ending very soon.

More to keep occupied than for financial reasons, I had taken on some private editing work, but I wasn't in the mood that week. It seemed all my energy was need-ed to keep from eating things I shouldn't eat, and that, of course, made me feel pitiful. A wave of anger washed over me. What did Rinpoche know about diet-ing? From the day I'd met him he'd eaten only with the greatest attention and gratitude, consuming my sister's earthy, bland concoctions, steering clear of processed foods, eschewing alcohol and sweets almost entirely, being served what my daughter, Natasha, called his "bird portion". He was completely in control of the workings of his mind—decades of meditation will do that for you, I suppose—so what right did he have to be running a weight-loss clinic for people whose minds betrayed them at every turn? He was duping us, this line of logic went, not for money, but out of some kind of spiritual egotism, to make himself feel righteous, to support the notion that he knew better, that he could teach us, base mortals that we were.

Such was the run of thoughts, the shape of my own bitchiness, to use Edna's word. I decided to go into the city I loved and see a movie, one of my preferred methods of distraction since Jeannie's death. I drove to the train station, caught an express to Grand Central, and found an empty seat. But halfway there a woman got on and sat beside me and once she settled in she opened a bag with a delicious-smelling prosciutto and provolone croissant sandwich. Worse, she would occasionally emit a small moan after a particularly satisfying bite.

"Smells good," I said, half-hoping she'd break off a piece and offer it to me and I'd have no option but to accept.

"They have this new bakery in town," she said happily. "Oscar's. If you live anywhere near here, you have to try it. Homemade bread to die for, and if you ask they'll just cut you a slice and slather it with butter and let you eat it right there with a cup of the best coffee you've ever tasted!"

You're some kind of devil-spirit, I wanted to tell her. You're a demon, set here beside me by the same forces that put the serpent in the Garden of Eden. But what I actually said was, "Sounds truly marvelous," and I opened my Times and pretended to read.

In the theater, naturally, the people behind me kept passing a bucket of buttered popcorn back and forth. I could smell it as clearly as if they were holding it beneath my nose. Popcorn wasn't off-limits, so I went back down to the lobby and returned with a large bucket, enough for four. Somehow, though it filled and overfilled my stomach, the urge to eat my forbidden fruit remained. The film itself didn't help: there were four or five or eight scenes of meals, all of them lovingly depicted, the actors chewing, mmmm-ing, the pasta and garlic bread shown in luxurious close-up, the desserts sugary and dripping.

Outside, afterwards, pretzel vendors materialized on every corner, as if they knew I was an enormous fan of the New York City pretzel (though I cannot bear mass-produced, bagged pretzels).

The whole thing was a torment. I called Edna; she didn't answer. I pictured her on her bed after having given in to temptation, lying there, burping, swathed in guilt.

I found a Vietnamese restaurant I liked and ordered fresh rolls, and the largest Pho on the menu. Egg noodles, not wheat. Massive amounts of vegetables. Enough broth to fill the belly of a rhinoceros. While waiting to be served I studied the waitstaff and hostess, not an ounce of fat among them, not one blessed ounce. That was the answer then: move to Vietnam. If I could just avoid the Vietnamese iced coffee with its condensed milk, or even if I could limit myself to one a day, and sweat it off strolling the hot streets of Ho Chi Minh City at noon. . . .

My mind was a circus. I walked out, full-bellied but decidedly, perversely, unsatisfied. It was wheat I wanted—bread, pizza crusts with the burnt bubbles, a good, rich, fresh, delicious raspberry muffin. I hurried to the train station and made it back to the relative safety of my house, only to find Rinpoche there, grinning as if he knew exactly the torment I was enduring and was about to assure me it was all part of some larger plan. My suffering would lead me to a svelter Otto and then, eventually, to enlightenment.

- 9 -

For the next three days we ate salads for dinner, poached eggs and two flimsy strips of bacon for breakfast, a lot of fruit at lunch. I wanted to scream at him. I sneaked a look at the scale and found that my weight loss had stalled at 6.5 pounds. 6.5 pounds after all that misery! Finally, on the night before our seventh meeting, I could bear it no longer and I said, "Rinpoche, we have to talk."

He was, of course, amenable. In fact, over the years of our acquaintance, I had never known a time when Rinpoche wasn't available for conversation, advice, help of any kind. The only thing he was even a tiny bit selfish about was his meditation practice, and he'd be flexible even with that, getting up earlier for his sitting time if, for example, the family had a trip planned to celebrate a birthday.

We sat in my living room, a comfortable place of leather sofas and family photos, a large TV screen against one wall, a million memories calling to me from the oak trim and Kashmirian carpet. A million, five million, ten million. Without the slightest effort I could recall my wife playing on the floor with our children, the dolls, the electric trains, the sick days home from school, the Christmas decorations, the high school friends sleeping over. And, more painfully, Jeannie lying ill on the sofa where Rinpoche now decided to settle himself.

I'd made us cups of herbal tea, and set out slices of apple and Jarlsberg cheese—his favorite. I sat opposite him in an armchair and suddenly lost my nerve. It seemed impossible to be angry at him at that moment. How could you be angry at love?

Still, I knew myself well enough by then to realize that holding dissatisfactions inside would only give them fuel. So, after a bit of chewing and sipping and bearing the weight of my famous brother-in-law's expectant gaze, I said, "I've gotten to a point where your weight loss regime is causing me some difficulty."

"What means this 'ree-jeem', Otto."

"A program, a way of doing things. In this case the program you designed for all of us."

"Ah." The pleasant gaze, the open face, the relaxed posture. Was there a man who felt more at ease in his own skin? "Not easy for you, maybe," he suggested.

"Not at all. Right now, especially. The first week wasn't too bad. The weeks after that were okay. But now I seem to have hit a wall. . . .to have gotten to a place where it's harder, not easier. And I'm really not losing that much weight. I stood on the scale today—against your rules, forgive me. Six and a half pounds in six weeks."

"Ah."

"I guess I expected more for my sacrifices. And I don't think I'm alone."

He broke eye contact, pursed his lips, and nodded in a serious way. "You listening to the other rules?"

"Yes. Even more than the rules. Instead of giving up one food I gave up a whole category. Wheat. And then alcohol as a secondary food. I meditate anyway, you know that. I walk, I get up and swing my arms and do deep-knee bends. Six and a half pounds!"

"Not about losing pounds," he said.

"No? I think the people who are left in your clinic would be pretty surprised to hear that statement."

He pondered this for a moment, seemed to register my tone, and then asked, "Where the pounds come from?"

"From an imbalance between calories in and calories out, with some consideration for metabolism and God knows what else." My anger was bubbling near the surface and I very nearly added: everyone knows that!

"Where the imbalance come from?"

"I just told you."

"I mean, where it start, this imbalance?"

"Who knows? It's different for everyone, I'd guess. We all—"

"No, same for everyone."

"With all respect, Rinpoche, I feel like you're making something very complicated and difficult sound simple and easy. It may very well be easy for you, but for the rest of us—"

"Seed of trouble same for everyone," he insisted.

"How so?"

"Mind."

"How so?"

"Mind tell you: eat, eat. Or: rest, rest. Or: too tired to exercise today. Or: had a bad time today so I can drink too much wine. Or: doin' good so far so I can eat the five cookies."

"Yes, but—"

"Other program, other ree-jeem, they focus on no sugar, or no bread, or exercise wery hard. Okay, not bad, this ree-jeem. But imbalance starts in mind, and if you don't fix mind, you don't fix problem no matter what you don't ever eat."

"It's not that simple."

"I think maybe is."

"The mind is so massively complicated. I mean, some people go into therapy for decades, trying to sort out their motivations and moods, their 'thought-patterns' you would say."

"Yes," he said, as if in complete agreement. And then, "this work for people?"

"For some people it does. We had friends whose lives were radically changed by therapy."

"They lose weight?"

"I don't know that any of them went with that in mind. I can't say."

"Therapy could help sometime, sure," he said. "But Rinpoche's way, I think, help a little faster. A little more straight."

"I've always thought ten weeks was, forgive me, a ridiculously short amount of time in which to see any real results."

"You not satisfy with six pound?"

I took refuge in a piece of cheese. I was, in fact, partially satisfied. Six pounds, as my barber Eddie used to say, "wasn't nothing." But the seeds of that evening's argument weren't planted in rational soil.

"Let me ask you one thing," Rinpoche said.

"Anything."

"Meditation help you all these years?"

"Absolutely. Without it I think I would have ceased to have even the slightest desire to live after Jeannie. . . after all that's happened. It's helped me with anger, with depression, with procrastination, with grief. I think of it as a kind of magic."

"Good." He got up from the couch and went over to the Webster's Dictionary that had stood on a side table from the time Natasha and Anthony were in grade school. He grunted when he lifted it—strictly for show; he was a powerful man—carried it back to his place on the sofa and opened it to about a third of the way through the thousand-some pages. He looked up at me and pinched those three hundred pages between thumb and forefinger. "This how far we gone, you and me, with the meditation." He grabbed the larger chunk. "This how far we need to go to put together the Relative and Absolute, to be little bit like Buddha, like Jesus."

"That's depressing."

"Opposite of depressing," he said. "Every the time you fix something in yourself—a little of anger, a little of the protastination—you turn one page." He turned a page. "Some pages more harder to turn. They don't go so easy, okay?"

"Okay."

"For some people, turning the page for the weight wery easy. No problem, man. No big imbalance. Maybe good metabolism, maybe just when they have a bad day they don't think about the food. Maybe something else is comfort for them, drugs, the sex, work, talk. For you and the other people is food. We working in ten weeks to turn one page, not all the pages for weight. One page. We trying break one habit, even break it little bit. Once you really break it in the mind, she stays breaked, okay?"

"People slip back."

"Sure. I know. I slip back in some things, too, Otto. Meditation things, different levels in meditation."

"I've never seen that."

"Inwisible," he said, staring hard at me. "Is part of life, this slipping back. Part of to be human. Like climbing on the mountain. But sometimes in the climbing when you really get up on a, how you say?" He ran one hand parallel to the floor, a sideways karate-chop.

"A ledge, a plateau."

"A edge, then you stay there always, you don't slip, okay? I trying now to get those people and you to the edge, not the top of the mountain."

"The ledge."

40

"Right, yes. You see?"

"I do see," I told him, and I did. "I'm sorry."

"What for, sorry? Eat the tea now, Otto my good friend, my brother-in-waw. One meeting soon other people say what you said, and I say what I said, and makes the ree-jeem better. Thank you, my good friend!"

- 10 -

I waited for Rinpoche to open up the next meeting to the kind of discussion we'd had that night—I suppose I wanted to hear that the others were struggling, too, and wanted him to defend his Webster's Dictionary model of spiritual growth in front of the group's more cynical members—but he ran meetings seven, eight, and nine, at the close of the brutal weeks six, seven, and eight, with an atypical curtness. He seemed not in a mood to entertain our complaints, though the room was fairly bubbling with them. Two more people quit and, though the vise wasn't tightened further—we stayed at two foods, two meditations, 1.5 miles walking and 88% portions (he did say we could weigh ourselves)—the difficulty of carrying something increases exponentially with the distance it is carried, and I believe we all felt that.

We were all suffering. Even a fairly trim, thirtyish couple (his name was Matt; she called him "Poochy", in public) could be heard post-meeting saying how much harder things got after the first two or three pounds.

"At first he was like my uncle," Poochy said. "Now he's a drill sergeant. He hasn't smiled in weeks."

A slight exaggeration. Still, Rinpoche's mini-sermons had taken on a decidedly no-nonsense air. He talked about self-discipline, and said that, while some people had more of it than others, it could be cultivated ("growed" was the word he used). You couldn't grow it out of a cluttered mind, so he suggested we watch a little less TV, cut back on Facebook and other on-line enjoyments, do one thing at a time, with full concentration.

"He's stripping us of all distraction," Edna complained over the phone. "When I turn off the TV the first thing I want to do is eat!"

"We're in the heat of battle now," I said, to console her, and myself. "A couple more weeks and we'll be going out for pizza."

"And ice cream," she said, and paused. "Even saying the words makes it harder these days, Otto."

- 11 -

But then, true to his promise, at the next-to-the-last meeting, Rinpoche did give a talk that re-sembled the conversation we'd had. And, true to his predictions, some people did say something like what I'd said. Though in much less gentle form. Of the fifteen who attended that meeting, by my count only six of them were pleased with the program, and with their progress. To my surprise, Edna was one of them. I remained neutral and quiet. The other eight were, in various forms, disappointed.

As he so often did, Obnoxious Joe led the charge. "Here we are," he said, the second after Rinpoche fin-ished his talk and opened the floor to questions, "nine damn weeks into a ten-week program for which I, for one, am gonna pay good money I can't really afford, and, dammit, I've gone by the rules and I've lost three pounds. Three! I need to lose thirty-three, Rinpoche! You seem like a nice man, but I have to say this is in-creasingly looking like a scam."

I expected Rinpoche to ask what 'scam' meant, but he only looked at Joe attentively, patiently, hearing him out.

"I'm glad I didn't bring my wife along, that's all I

can say. We have one more meeting after this and un-less some miracle happens in these seven days I would like to ask to be excused from paying."

"Me, too," a woman beside him said.

Rinpoche nodded. Joe sat back down, muttering so persistently that Poochy turned around and told him to shut up.

"Easy for you, Mister Slim!" Joe hissed.

"No, it isn't. It isn't easy for anyone!"

Edna got to her feet. "Well," she said, "I guess you can put me in the other camp. It's true I haven't lost massive amounts of weight, but then I really didn't ex-pect that to happen in ten weeks. I have lost fifteen pounds, which is something."

Two women at the back of the room applauded.

"And I do feel like I've started to change the way I approach food, and also the way I approach eating and exercise. Giving up the two foods has helped me pay more attention to what I put into my body. And I do feel like that's going to benefit me in the long run. Ben-efit me in a way that none of the other things I've tried have done."

We went back and forth that way for fifteen minutes, a few people venting anger, a few meekly dis-satisfied, a few silent, a couple of others in Edna's camp, men and women who were beginning to feel that something had changed in them.

Rinpoche allowed them all as much time as they wanted, and then he said, "I been thinking about this and I decided everybody gets to pay no money. If you want to pay we put it in a bag and we carrying it down to the place where they feed the people who have hungry."

One of the women in the back of the room started to object, to say she wanted to pay, it had been worth it to her, she insisted on paying, it was much cheaper than other programs she'd tried. But Rinpoche held up one hand and went on. I thought for a moment he'd apologize for the whole clinic, admit it had been a mistake, that he didn't have any qualifications and had only been trying to do good in the world, to ease a burden he saw so many Americans carrying. But what he said was, "Now for last week the rules like this: you stay giving up your first food but you can eat little bit of your second if you want. You stay walking. You stay meditating, but try maybe ten minutes two times in a day or even a little more if you can. Not too much, but maybe a little more. And when you eat, you eat slow, that's all. Finish the chewing before you put more in, okay?"

"I expected something really hard for the last week," Edna said. "I expected some big challenge."

"Big challenge gonna be after next week," Rinpoche told her, and for the first time in weeks he broke into his familiar chuckle, as if all the criticism, all of Obnoxious Joe's vitriol had flown out one of the tall windows and into the mild March day. "Otto," he pointed to me, "goin' to write up all the rules for after next week. No new rules. But you goin' to have this piece of paper from Otto to remind you and the challenge gonna be to follow those rules much as you can when we finished. When Rinpoche not here."

He asked if there were any more questions or comments and, since there weren't, the meeting broke up. People stood and stretched, small conversations—pleasant and not-so-pleasant—bloomed at the edges of the room. Obnoxious Joe could be heard going on and on about the money—until his listener reminded him that Rinpoche was going to give us the program for free. Even that didn't seem to quiet him, though. Besides being addicted to food, Obnoxious Joe, it seemed, was addicted to feeling cheated.

I was folding the chairs and leaning them against the back wall, as I always did. Edna came over with one chair held horizontal in front of her. A bit out of breath from the exertion, she placed it against the others and stood facing me. "I have something to ask that I couldn't ask on the phone," she said. Her large, pretty face was troubled, vulnerable, the cheeks moving in small spasms, the eyes holding me.

"Sure, Edna, anything."

"I wanted to ask you to come to my place for dinner. I'm going to cook. It will be perfectly healthy, no worries about that. And it's going to be good, too, just some kind of meat and a vegetable and maybe my special sauce, and some fruit. No rules will be broken, but I wanted you to see where I live, and I wanted to cook for you. You've been so helpful to me."

"You don't have to do that, Edna. You've been as helpful to me as I've been to —"

"I really want to," she said, and of course I agreed.

- **12** -

After her husband died and her sons left the nest, Edna had moved from the family home in West New York to a twentieth-floor, two-bedroom condominium in a new apartment building in Jersey City. I found it—a gleaming structure of blue glass and steel—without any trouble, and carried an expensive bottle of Barolo up in the elevator. Alcohol had been my second 'food', and I'd done a good job avoiding it, but, because for the final week of the clinic Rinpoche had loosened the restrictions, I'd purchased the wine without guilt and brought it along. Edna had asked me if beef—"lean beef, Otto"—and asparagus would be okay for the meal, and I'd said yes, of course, I was an omnivore and ate everything that was put in front of me.

On the way up in the elevator I was thinking about that answer, thinking it had probably touched a sore spot with her. And then I thought about how many sore spots there must be for a woman like Edna, how many times in the course of a day someone said something—on TV, or radio, in her classes or her office—that knocked her back into a shame-filled self-consciousness, a kind of self-hatred, really. Something I knew only in its mildest form.

I was thinking, too, about what a nice friendship we'd developed, how comfortable I felt with her. There was a particular kind of intimacy involved in the public sharing of one's shameful precincts. I'd never been to an AA or NA meeting, but I imagined that, if you went there and unburdened yourself in complete sincerity, and watched others do the same, then it must be a kind of antidote to the daily communal circus in which, to one degree or another, we all appeared in disguise, played a role, put our best face forward. So many of us were addicted, depending on how broadly you defined the word. What a deep relief to let a bit of light shine into that cavern. In some ways I felt closer to Edna than to the men and women I'd worked with at Stanley and Byrnes for decades, all of us acting upbeat and confident, when, in fact, as I had discovered, we were as easily broken as a dry twig.

And we were so quick to judge, too, I thought, stepping out into a tiled hallway. Who knew what crushing blows had sent strong men onto the sidewalk on Eighth Avenue? Who knew what pain the woman pounding down donuts in the coffee shop was carrying?

I tapped on the door and Edna answered in an elegant, sky-blue dress with flowers embroidered along the low neckline. She gave me a warm, quick hug, admired the wine. Behind her I could see a table set with candles and sparkling china, and I noticed, too, in the

last of the afternoon light, that her dining room windows offered a view toward the downtown Manhattan
skyline. From what I could see of her place—kitchen,
dining room/living room—it was spotlessly clean,
framed photos of her children on the side-table, Spole-
to prints on the walls.

"You've been to Italy?"

She nodded, then bent over to take a sizzling sirloin
of beef from the oven. "Twice, with Ron. Once before
we had children, once for our twentieth. I noticed, the
second time especially, how few obese people there
were, and yet everyone seemed to eat like famished ox-
en after a day in the fields."

"A mystery."

"Yes, but let's not talk about food and weight and
such things tonight, if you don't mind."

"Absolutely."

I asked if I could help. She refused and told me to
go look out the window. I loved that view, from all an-
gles, from the Henry Hudson when I drove in, from
Brooklyn Heights when I visited friends, through the
windshield as I drove up the Jersey Turnpike. The sky-
scrapers seemed to me to have been built on a founda-
tion of some crazy American optimism. So much could
have gone wrong in the planning and construction—
faulty materials or design, unstable ground, a miscalcu-
lated cantilever—and yet there they stood, decade after
decade, tribute to a particular kind of genius and a per-
sistent hope: that the world would go on, that people
would work, and eat, and live, in the face of war and

weather, crises of one sort and another. Generations had passed away; with two famous exceptions, the buildings remained.

The meal was sumptuous and simple: perfectly-cooked, high-quality beef, tender spears of asparagus with just a bit of butter flavoring them. No bread. No starch. We sat across from each other, between the candles, enjoying the wine, and we talked about our families, where our children had flown off to, what they were doing. I noticed that Edna was making a concerted effort to eat slowly, to chew thoughtfully, not to put anything into her mouth until it was empty, but we succeeded in not talking about Rinpoche's clinic or his advice.

"It wouldn't be a meal without coffee and dessert," she surprised me by saying, when we were finished. "Decaf okay? And the dessert is fresh raspberries dusted with a little powdered sugar. About as harmless a thing as I could imagine."

"Perfect," I said. "And it was a delicious meal."

Pleasant as everything had been—the food and wine, the conversation—when we were most of the way through the final course a somewhat difficult silence descended upon us. At the first touch of it I wanted to fill the void with talk. That was my usual strategy in awkward moments: make a joke, tell a story, ask a question I knew would require a thoughtful answer. But for whatever reason I refrained from doing that with Edna. The silence was awkward, yes, but not miserably so. We concentrated on spooning up the last berries, emptying our coffee cups, avoiding each other's eyes. When the plates were clean and there was no other escape, I said, "I am a consummate dishwasher, you know. One of the best in Westchester County from all accounts."

She looked up and smiled. Something, some small trouble, skittered across her lips. "Well, it's true you shouldn't jump right back in your car after half a bottle of wine, but I could never let you wash dishes. That's part of my exercise routine, for one thing—all that standing—and it would be rude. My mother would turn over in her grave. I'd rather just give you a tour—some nice framed photos from Italy in the other rooms—and maybe we can sit and talk for a while."

It was only at that moment that I sensed a new kind of tension between us. My excuse is that I'd been out of the dating world for more than half my life. Since Jeannie's passing I'd had a few lunch conversations with women friends, some of them single, but the idea of doing anything more than talking with them had never entered even the outermost orbits of my mind. But something in Edna's tone of voice awakened that dormant instinct, something in her expression, the idea of getting a tour, when, unless there was another, hidden floor to the apartment with a library, servants, and leather armchairs, the only place we could tour were the bedrooms. In truth, until that moment, I hadn't thought of her in sexual terms, not consciously, at least. She was beautiful, yes. And there was the above-mentioned sense of intimacy between us. But the truth is that, by inclination or because of a lifetime of societal propaganda, I had never made any erotic connection, mentally, with women who looked like her, who were shaped like her, who were. . . fat.

What changed that, I don't know. Not the wine, assuredly. Not any sense of pity at how hurt she might be if I suddenly remembered I had an imaginary dentist appointment the next morning, first thing, and ought to be getting on my way, but what a wonderful meal it had been, what a nice conversation, and so on. Not even my own loneliness. It wasn't any of that. In fact, in the second when I said, "I'd like to see them" and stood up from the table, the attraction I felt did not belong to the world of the body at all, but to some other realm. And when we'd started our tour with a quick glance at a photograph she'd taken on the outskirts of Florence, at a country inn there, and then she'd turned to me and I put my hands on the outsides of her arms and leaned in and kissed her, we stepped into a world of such spiritual nakedness, such emotional ease, that it seemed we'd been best friends since childhood.

There was physical pleasure, yes, for both of us. In bed, in the dark, without clothes, Edna seemed to reach a level of comfort with her own body that escaped her in the walking-around hours. It was an infectious comfort. There was something decidedly sexy about it, a lack of hurry, an astonishing lack of self-doubt. It was more than fun; it was a joining of spirits, a mutual trust. Lesser cousin to long-time love.

Afterwards we lay quiet for a time in what Jackson

Brown once called, "the ruins of our pleasure", though perhaps "ruin" is the wrong word for what I felt. After a long silence, during which I found myself wondering if I might have made a mistake, led her to envision a relationship for which I wasn't ready, Edna said, "That was so nice." And then, "I hope you don't think I had this planned all along, because I didn't. Until I was in the kitchen putting the sugar on the berries I didn't really think of it at all."

"If that's an apology," I said. "It's completely and totally unnecessary. If it's an expression of regret, I'm hurt."

She laughed. She said, "Well, nice as it was, you're really not my type if you want to know the truth. Too skinny. So you don't have to worry that I'm in love or anything. I know how men are."

I took it as she'd meant it, on all its various levels, and I got dressed in the darkness of the room, unworried. Edna lay on the bed, apparently exhausted. I leaned down for a last kiss, and drove home in a bath of a kind of peace so unfamiliar to me that I could not give it a name.

- 13 -

The final meeting of Rinpoche's Remarkable Ten-Week Weight Loss Clinic was a weird mix of festive and furious. Edna, two other women, and one of the men brought him bouquets of flowers. Obnoxious Joe, his partner in whinery, Mad Matilda, and three members of what I thought of as the "Cohort of Complaint" sat together grumpily in the third of three rows of chairs. With the flowers on the table beside his cup of tea, Rinpoche began the proceedings by saying: "I talk enough now, in these ten week. Your turn now. Say what you want and then afterward we try one thing."

It took approximately a second and a half for Obnoxious Joe to get to his feet and begin. "I've decided," he said, in a tone of voice overflowing with the desire to be The One Who Is Listened To, an affliction I'd come across in other audience members at Rinpoche's many talks, "to make the payment in spite of my anger." He waved a check in the air. "You said last time it was going to the Food Pantry. That's a good cause, so I made it out that way, rather than to you. And it's a tax deduction!" His cohort laughed; the rest of us just watched, waiting for him to cede the floor. "I've followed your rules, Rinpoche, and lost exactly four pounds in ten weeks, so this is obviously a scam or, at the very least, a display of the ego of someone who wants, not only to be famous for spiritual books, but to be a weight-loss guru, besides. Be that as it may, here's my check and I'll be happy not to have to waste any more time coming here after this meeting ends."

If it is possible to describe the act of sitting down as having anger in it, that was the case with our Joe. I had to bite the inside of my cheek to keep from calling across the room: If it wasn't working for you, then why did you keep coming all these weeks?

Mad Matilda got to her feet next. "I'm with Joe," she said, "except I'm not as nice as he is and I don't care about tax deductions and I've decided not to pay. I'll make a donation to my own charity of choice, thank you. I've heard so many good things about you, Rinpoche, but I hope you never do anything like this ever again."

The other three people in the back row went through the motion of applauding without making any noise, but said nothing.

There was a bad pause during which I expected Rinpoche to respond. He didn't. The windows were open, letting in the first hopeful breezes of spring. He sat with his robe hanging down around his ankles, he took a sip of tea, he blinked a few times, but the assault didn't seem to have any measurable effect on him. Doubt, I'd noticed many times over the years, was an alien concept to Volya Rinpoche. In the long course of our acquaintance I'd wondered, at moments, if that was supposed to be the end point of the spiritual path—a deeply-rooted confidence, or if he was laboring under some kind of self-delusion, an unwillingness to consider the idea that he might actually be mistaken. I don't mean to make him out to be conceited: that's the last word you'd use with him. He was just so sure. If he made a small mistake, misremembered something, pointed the car in the wrong direction on a trip, he'd admit it. But I'm talking here about the larger issues, questions of judgment, of ethics, of morality, of meaning. He never seemed shaken by those, and he wasn't shaken then either. It felt like Joe and his pals could step to the front of the room and hit Rinpoche over the head with the folding chairs and he'd blink, breathe, wait for it to be finished and then move on. I wondered if he and my sister had ever once had a real, knock-down, drag-out spousal spat. Watching him endure the slings and arrows of the Cohort of Complaint, that possibility seemed to fall somewhere on the spectrum between highly unlikely and absolutely impossible.

As I somehow suspected she would, Edna stood up into that silence, into the echo of those insults. I remembered the feeling of her body in bed and I watched to see if, after her ten weeks of work, she might be moving easier. It did seem that she was. A bit easier.

Edna cleared her throat, sent a wicked glance back and sideways at the Cohort of Complaint, and then turned to Rinpoche. "I have to admit," she began, "that for a while there I was thinking the same things you've just heard. I was surprised at first at the way you structured this clinic, and then disappointed, but little by little I've been coming around to the idea that maybe you're way ahead of us, way ahead of the thousands of diet gurus and the authors of books and the people who run other clinics like this. As you said last time—and this made a big impression on me—it's not really about the food, it's about the mind, the kind of habitual thinking that's gotten us into this predicament in the first place. I have trouble with the meditations, I admit that. But I keep doing them, and once in a while now I can catch the very beginning of the urge that makes me eat things I shouldn't eat. Not every time. I still slip. But once in a while I can see that little devil, and sometimes when I see it I have the will to stop myself. My partner here," she gestured sideways to me, and then rested a hand on my shoulder for a couple of seconds, "has been unbelievably helpful, and I think your partner system was really smart, the best part of the whole clinic. I lost a total of sixteen pounds, Rinpoche. And it was brutal. I need to lose five times that much to regain any semblance of appreciation for my physical self. But sixteen pounds is a lot in ten weeks, and it's better than I've done before, ever, in lots and lots of trying, and I have the feeling that maybe, just maybe, I can use what you've taught me and slowly go further along the good road. So thank you."

"Welcome," Rinpoche said.

There was a quiet muttering from the Cohort end

of the room. We waited for someone else to stand and, at last, someone did. Everything about this man was round—round face, round neck, round shoulders, round thighs—and I guessed he was at the upper end of that middle category, carrying forty or maybe fifty extra pounds. He'd never before said a word in the meetings, never joined in the post-meeting complaint and camaraderie. "I'm Jose," he said. "Half Mexican, half White. I was abused as a boy. Very bad. Been in therapy ten years, been tryin' to lose weight thirty years. Been addicted to different things—drugs, booze, prostitutes. Did a little time for something small." He paused there and I realized, after a moment, that there were tears on his face. But his voice went on without breaking. "I'll never be that thin, muscular guy you see on TV. That will never happen. And probably I'll never really heal, you know, completely. I signed up for this only because my girlfriend, who's nice and slim, read one of your books and told me you know some things. I didn't feel like I was wasting my time here. I listened to everything you said. I did what you told us to do. I even did the meditation part, which helped me more when I got off the chair than when I was on it. I think therapy is good for some people. I still go. I think meetings are good. But," he turned at looked at Joe and I worried for a second he was going to challenge him to a brawl in the alleyway next to the building, "I think this was good, too. I lost some weight, sure. But I think just really trying hard made me feel better about myself. Just that. And it made me feel close to the people here.

Most of them. I remember the thing you said on day one, about us being perfect on some level. Sometimes when I make love with my girlfriend I feel that. And one time when I was meditating at home I felt that. For about two minutes. And when I got up from meditating I kept feeling it for a while. Then it went away. Nothing like that ever happened to me before in my life. Maybe it will never happen again. But I won't forget it. For two minutes, without sex or booze or drugs, I felt, you know, all right about myself for the first time in thirty years. So thank you."

When Jose sat down I thought the room might erupt into applause, but that would have been a scene from reality TV, and this was reality without the TV. You could hear the hurt in Jose's voice, and see it on his wet face, but it didn't make you want to applaud. It did, however, make The Cohort stop muttering. Most people were looking at Jose, or at the floor, and then, as if Rinpoche were reading my mind, he said, "I make lot of jokes. I laugh all a time. Sometimes some people they get bothered from this. Why can I be laughing when so much pain in this world? Good question." He started to laugh again but stopped himself in mid-chuckle. "When I come to America first time I see a lot of big people, you know," he stretched his arms out to the side.

"It's okay to call us fat," a woman called out.

Rinpoche smiled at her. "Big," he said again. "Too much big. When I see this I see pain. Different kinds, maybe. Some from long time ago, like this good man,

Jose. Some new. I think: what I can do about this pain?
So I say, let me try this thing, this clinic. Let me give
the meditation to big people, see if it works. Now we
goin' to do one different meditation and then we'll be
finish and if you want to put money here on this table
you can and I'll bring it to the hungry people, and if
you don't want to, no problem for Rinpoche. We do
this meditation, then we say good-bye, okay? Thank
you for coming."

"Thank you!" a few people called out.

Rinpoche nodded. "I want to say, before we get to
the meditation, one more last thing. This thing important. We are not here about—how you call it?—this
'fat'. We are not here about food. Food not the most
important part. Maybe the word for why we are here is
a wery hard word. 'Addiction' is that word. What is this
addiction?"

He took a sip of tea and, at that moment, to my
astonishment, Obnoxious Joe yelled out, "You're addicted to tea, Rinpoche. I can see it!"

Rinpoche looked at him, waited one beat to be
sure, then smiled. "You made the joke," he said. "Wery
good!"

"Thank you."

"Maybe you not so mad now."

"Not really. Still mad. Still disappointed. But I have
three sisters who are addicts, three out of four, so I'm
interested to hear this last word. And I didn't want
people to think I'm obnoxious."

Too late, I almost said, but I just watched him. He

was truly what Natasha would have called an 'odd duck', and I imagined him going from one weight-loss scheme to the next, gulping dissatisfaction, belching complaints.

"Sorry for your sisters," Rinpoche said. His eyebrows went up and down once. "What is this addiction?" he asked, looking at Joe. Joe didn't answer, so Rinpoche went on. "Is something you do again and again and again but you don't want to. Or maybe you want to but you know, some level, is no good for you. Wery interesting. Why we do this?"

No one offered an answer.

"I think the reason maybe because addiction has good friends with pain."

"*Is* good friends with pain," someone corrected him.

"Maybe is like brother or a sister with pain. A siblin'. Anytime you see addiction, you see pain is close by. What takes away the pain sometimes is the love, but maybe the addicted person too ashamed for this love, doesn't want it, doesn't let it inside, hurts other people sometime to keep away this love. So in this meditation now we do the opposite. We let love come to us. We sit and we remember somebody who loved us wery much! Maybe was father, mother, brother, sister, wife, husband, daughter, son, best friend, doesn't matter. We remember this person, this love. Anytime our mind goes away, we come back to this feeling that someone loves us. We remember it. We feel it. A simple meditation—maybe you can laugh at—but I ask for you to watch how many things get in the way, how many times we feel that love was no good, we didn't deserve, isn't real. Or maybe we can't find somebody and we have to imagine, maybe a God who love us. Jesus, maybe. Buddha. Sometimes we feel like even Buddha and Jesus can't love us, yes?"

"Yes!" someone said.

"Okay. Just keep watching. Keep coming back to that feeling that somebody loves you. Maybe seems too simple but I think is worth a little try. Just this one time. If it doesn't work, don't keep doing it later on, okay? And I this time forgotted my bell." He reached into the folds of his robe and produced, as if by magic, a fork. "At the end when I hit the cup, stay with your eyes closed for maybe another few seconds and then we're all finish here and I hope you have every blessing in this life and beyond this life. Thank you."

Rinpoche tapped fork against tea cup. I closed my eyes and for a minute or so searched around in my memory for a source of love. There was, in my life, no shortage of sources, but, strangely enough, after that minute was over I settled on my late dog, Jasper, a Doberman/Lab mix who had graced us with his presence for thirteen years. On what turned out to be his last night on earth we'd let him up on the sofa—an unusual treat and we'd had to help him up there—and he laid his head sideways on my thigh. By then it was difficult for him to breathe. Each inhalation was accompanied by a small grunt. Clearly he was in pain. But, and this will be no surprise to dog owners, there was, at the same time, a perfect trust. In me. A perfect acceptance. As if he were the incarnation of Buddhism's Absolute View and saw me as being a man without blemish. As if there were no other master he'd want to entrust with his safety in his final hours, as if he asked nothing and was ready to give everything. I told myself to remember to ask Rinpoche for the Buddhist explanation: what spiritual purpose did pets serve on this earth?

I supposed I knew the answer, but what an answer it was! How strange that, in a society where people found it so difficult to believe they were lovable, there should be so many pets.

My mind drifted this way and that. What a foolish thing, some voice said, choosing a dog. Why not choose your wife, your children? Your mother or father? I didn't try to answer that voice, or to make any logical connection between my dog's love and eating. I just did what Rinpoche had instructed us to do: returned to that feeling of being loved, returned there against all the modern world's obstacles and objections.

He hadn't specified a time for our last meditation. We were certainly past the ten-minute mark, then past fifteen-minutes. I was aware of people shifting positions, a few coughs. Someone stood up and sat down again. Twenty minutes at least and I kept coming back to that feeling of being loved. I kept coming back to Jasper. I wasn't thinking about it, or analyzing it. I wasn't worried about what my sophisticated Manhattan friends might think about the meditation. I just kept remembering my dog in his last hours on earth.

And then the fork sounded against Rinpoche's cup. I opened my eyes. Edna reached over and put a hand on my thigh. "Who'd you think about?" she asked, and for a moment I worried she was wishing I'd thought about her, or was about to say she'd thought about me. Friendship was fine. The lovemaking had been better than fine. But I really didn't want to embark on another relationship just then.

"Be honest," she said, hopefully.

"My dog."

One beat, and then a huge smile broke across her lovely face. "That," she said, "is so perfect."

"You?"

"My grandmother. I'm going to do that meditation every day. And I'm going to call you whenever I feel like having a coffee milkshake."

"More often than that, I hope." And the smile broke across her face again and I put my hand over hers. She squeezed my leg once and took her hand away and, with some effort, got to her feet and went up to say a word of thanks to Volya Rinpoche. I folded the chairs and set them against the wall, watching her out of the corner of my eye.

As she was making her way toward the door, she came over and held me, for at least half a minute, in a warm embrace.

* * *

Two weeks later, as Rinpoche and I sat at Amadeo's, sipping our beers and waiting for our sausage and onion pizza to be served, my spiritual teacher said, in a casual way, "You had the nice partner for the clinic, yes?"

"Yes, Edna. Very fine woman. I believe it really helped her, too."

Rinpoche nodded, watching me. "You hear from her again now?"

"No. It's strange. I've written her a couple of times, called. No response. I even checked with the college where she teaches to make sure she hadn't had a heart attack or something. I left her a message there, too, but she doesn't seem to want to be in touch anymore. I'm puzzled. We were pretty close."

The pizza was carried to our table—the sausage glistening in a light coating of oil, the crust beautifully bubbled, just a bit of charred dough here and there. I separated four slices so they'd cool faster and then I actually licked my fingers.

"For some people is wery hard to feel a person love them," Rinpoche noted. "Some level, deep, they want to push the love away. Wery, how you say? Settle."

"Subtle, yes." I said, absent-mindedly. I took my first bite—almost as magnificent as I'd imagined.

And for a few seconds then, distracted by the ecstasy of eating, I thought Rinpoche had been talking about Edna.

Some Other Books by PFP / AJAR Contemporaries

a four-sided bed - Elizabeth Searle

A Russian Requiem - Roland Merullo

Ambassador of the Dead - Askold Melnyczuk

Blind Tongues - Sterling Watson

Celebrities in Disgrace (eBook version only) - Elizabeth Searle

Demons of the Blank Page - Roland Merullo

excerpts from Smedley's Secret Guide to World Literature -
Askold Melnyczuk

Fighting Gravity - Peggy Rambach

"Gifted: An Indestructibles Christmas Story"-
Matthew Phillion

Girl to Girl: The Real Deal on Being A Girl Today-Anne Driscoll

"Invitations: A Story of Thanksgiving" - Peter Sarno

"Last Call" (eBook "single") - Roland Merullo

Leaving Losapas - Roland Merullo

Lunch with Buddha - Roland Merullo

Make A Wish But Not For Money - Suzanne Strempek Shea

Music In and On the Air - Lloyd Schwartz

My Ground Trilogy - Joseph Torra

Passion for Golf: In Pursuit of the Innermost Game -
Roland Merullo

Revere Beach Boulevard - Roland Merullo

Revere Beach Elegy: A Memoir of Home & Beyond -
Roland Merullo

Taking the Kids to Italy - Roland Merullo

Talk Show - Jaime Clarke

Temporary Sojourner - Tony Eprile

the Book of Dreams - Craig Nova

The Calling - Sterling Watson

The Entropy of Everything: the Indestructibles Book 3 -
Matthew Phillion
The Family Business - John DiNatale
The Indestructibles - Matthew Phillion
The Indestructibles: Breakout - Matthew Phillion
The Italian Summer: Golf, Food, and Family at Lake Como -
Roland Merullo
The Return - Roland Merullo
*The Ten Commandments of Golf Etiquette: How to Make the Game
More Enjoyable for Yourself and for Everyone Else on the Course* -
Roland Merullo
*The Winding Stream: The Carters, the Cashes and the Course
of Country Music* - Beth Harrington
"The Young and the Rest of Us" *(eBook "single")* -
Elizabeth Searle
*This is Paradise: An Irish Mother's Grief, an African Village's
Plight and the Medical Clinic That Brought Fresh Hope to Both* -
Suzanne Strempek Shea
Tornado Alley - Craig Nova
"What A Father Leaves" (eBook "single" & audio book) -
Roland Merullo
What Is Told - Askold Melnyczuk

* * *

Coming Soon !

Beyond the Chandelier
a memoir by Steve Forbert

* * *